SENIE DENTON

Romantic Movie Classics

Contents

One

Introduction

Welcome to my book of lists of romantic movie classics. While doing my research for the book I learned that the first movie produced in Hollywood was The Count of Monte Cristo in 1908. I also learned there are 51 genres of movies. This particular bit of information just really caught me by surprise. So, for the purposes of this book , I am going to stick with romance and romantic comedy. I am going to begin in the 1940's with what I call classic films. The ones that mom and dad watched right after they got their first black and white tv. Then we are going to move through the decades and I will share with you some of my favorite ones and the ones that I love to watch over and over. So, sit back , relax , get your notepad and you can start your own list.

Two

Chapter 1 : The 1940's

The 1940's

This list of the 1940's is definitely on my bucket list , as I have only seen one of these movies. It's a Wonderful Life with James Stewart and Donna Reed in 1946 has become a Christmas tradition at my home. I watch it every year during the holidays and it never gets old. It always makes me feel warm and fuzzy on the inside and leaves a smile on my face.

- Philadelphia Story with Carey Grant, Katharine Hepburn and James Stewart. A socialite splits from her ex-husband and prepares to wed a wealthy, business man ,when the ex and another man cross paths with her and she finds herself wondering which one she loves.

- Casablanca with Ingrid Bergman and Humphrey Bogart. A nightclub owner has to decide if he is willing to help his ex-lover and her husband escape the Nazis in French Morocco.

-

- Rebecca with Lawrence Olivier and Joan Fontaine. In this Alfred HItchcock romance/thriller, a young woman who marries a wealthy widower, must learn how to live in the shadow of his wife, who mysteriously died.

-

- The Lady Eve with Barbara Stanwick and Henry Fonda. A brewery heir falls for a con artist trying to sink her claws into his fortune. When he catches on to her little game , he dumps her and then she is faced with the fact that she really is in love with him.

-

- Laura with Gene Tierney and Dana Andrews. A police detective falls in love with the suspected murderer.

-

- Notorious with Carey Grant and Ingrid Bergman. The daughter of a former Nazi spy is asked by the United States to spy on the Nazis herself.

-

- Arise My Love with Claudette Colbert and Ray Milland. A pilot and a reporter have a romantic adventure in Europe as the war begins to break out.

-

- Woman of the Year with Katharine Hepburn and Spencer Tracy. A political female writer meets her match at the paper they both work for. Not having much in common but opposites do attract, the two begin a romance and later marry. Everything is fine and dandy until she wins the Woman of the

Year award and he has to take back stage to her new popularity.

-

- Ball of Fire with Gary Cooper and Barbara Stanwyck. Sugarpuss, a burlesque singer, captivates an encyclopedia writer who shows up at the bar to do some research for his new chapter on slang words. She definitely has a way with them and he invites her to his home. Unbeknownst to him, she is the sweetheart of a mobster and now he has a target on his back.

-

- For Whom the Bell Tolls with Gary Cooper and Ingrid Bergman. An American travels abroad to fight against the dictator of Spain. His duties require him to blow up a bridge. Near the military base, he meets and falls in love with a young woman from Spain and he begins to question why he is really there.

Three

Chapter 2 : The 1950's

The 1950's

- **Roman Holiday with Audrey Hepburn and Gregory Peck.
  Audrey plays a crowned princess who is tired of being sur-
  rounded with her security and skips out of the embassy to
  tour Rome alone. She meets a reporter, Gregory Peck, and the
  two begin a romantic tour through this romantic city.**

-

- **An Affair to Remember with Carey Grant and Deborah Kerr.
  Two young people meet on a cruise and begin a romance, while
  each of them are engaged to other people.**

-

- **The African Queen with Humphrey Bogart and Katharine
  Hepburn. A missionary spinster, whose brother was killed
  while in Africa by the Germans, persuades a riverboat captain**

to use his own boat to destroy a German boat.

- A Star is Born with Judy Garland and James Mason. A rising new singer trying to break into the business is taken under the wing of an accomplished star, only to fall in love with her, see her career blossom and his' take a dive.

- Cat on a Hot Tin Roof with Paul Newman and Elizabeth Taylor. An ex-football player who has seen his career come to an end begins drinking and destroying his marriage. Then one day a reunion with his sick father brings back old memories and sheds light on new insights.

- Rebel Without a Cause with Natalie Wood, Sal Mineo and James Dean. A new troubled teenager comes to town in hopes of starting with a clean slate. He makes friends with some of the wrong people and makes enemies with others.

- Indiscreet with Carey Grant and Ingrid Bergman. A famous actress believes that she has missed her chance at love and marriage, so she decides to return to her home. She later attends a banquet with her sister and brother-in-law and sparks an interest in a man she meets there. A romance follows , only for her to learn he is a married man.

- The Long, Hot Summer with Joann Woodward and Paul Newman. A smooth con-man comes into town and soon finds the wealthiest plantation owner to attach to, seemingly working his way into the family business and falling for the daughter.

- **White Christmas with Danny Kaye , Bing Crosby, Rosemary Clooney. A singing pair of fellows hook up with a sisters' act and hold a benefit show to help save a Vermont Inn from going under. This is one movie you will watch many times during the Christmas season.**

Four

Chapter 3 : The 1960's

The 1960's

- **The Graduate with Dustin Hoffman, Katharine Ross and Anne Bancroft. A college graduate returns to his parents home to figure out what he wants to do with his life. During this time he is seduced by a married woman who is friends with his parents,only to later fall for the woman's daughter.**

-

- **Romeo and Juliet with Leonard Whiting and Olivia Hussey. Tragic romance between two young people who fall in love , in spite of the fact that their families are enemies.**

-

- **West Side Story with Natalie Wood, Rita Moreno, George Chakiris and Richard Beymer. Two young teens of rival street gangs begin a deadly turf war, when one of the members falls** in love with another member's sister.

•

• The Sound of Music with Julie Andrews and Christopher Plummer. This movie is based on the true story of the Von Trapp Family,from Austria, who were singers during World War II. The family escapes into Switzerland before the Nazis can overtake them. A young woman becomes a governess in the home of the family of seven children and the widowed father. This one is an absolute must see. Intertwined within this movie is tragedy of Austria losing it's country to the Nazis. This was the highest grossing film in 1965 and received five academy awards. The scenery and the music are just fabulous.

•

• Barefoot in the Park with Jane Fonda and Robert Redford. Young newlyweds live in a fifth floor walk-up apartment in New York City. As the woman tries to be a matchmaker for her single mom, the newlyweds soon get caught up in a comical argument which makes them question their own marriage.

•

• Doctor Zhivago with Omar Sharif and Julie Christie. Set during the Russian Revolution, a young doctor falls for a woman who is involved with an older man. The doctor later marries someone else, but years later crosses paths with her again and their love affair reignites.

•

• The Thomas Crown Affair with Steve McQueen and Faye Dunaway. A bored bank executive millionaire concocts the perfect bank heist and gets away with it. Confident that he can do it again he devises a new one, only to get romantically involved with a confident, sexy insurance investigator.

•

- **This property is Condemned with Natalie Wood, Robert Redford and Charles Bronson. During the Depression a young woman is pressured by her mother to marry a rich man, but she is in love with a younger man. The mother forces her to stop seeing the young man, so the young woman seeks revenge on her mother by starting a relationship with her mother's boyfriend.**

Five

Chapter 4 : The 1970's

The 1970's

- A Star is Born with Barbra Streisand and Kris Kristofferson. A remake of a 1930 and 1950's movie. A declining rock star , from alcohol and drugs, happens upon a new singer at a club and the two begin a romance. He slowly brings her on stage with him and her career explodes. As her career takes off, his is slowly declining and he returns to drinking again, as he can't handle her success over his own. It has a tragic outcome but a very emotional and fitting ending. The soundtrack is fabulous .

-

- The Great Gatsby with Robert Redford, Mia Farrow and Sam Waterston. This is a story about a mysterious millionaire who has gained great social status and wealth, but is still missing the one thing he has always longed for, his true love from his youth.

•

- Love Story with Ryan O'Neal and Ali Mcgraw. A romantic tear jerker where a wealthy Harvard student falls in love with a middle class girl. Through protests from her parents they have a beautiful love story until tragedy strikes. It is an absolute gem and a perfect love story , these two actors just warm your heart. One of the absolute best movies you will ever cry all the way through and want to watch it again.

•

- The Way We Were with Barbra Streisand and Robert Redford. A college romance that ends and then begins again years later between a politically active woman and a screenwriter . They fall in love, marry, then infidelity occurs and later a child is born, but the relationship just can't hold on. Just getting to look at Redford for hours is a joy. One of the best actors of all time in my opinion.

•

- Annie Hall with Woody Allen and Diane Keaton. A comedian reflects on his life with a nightclub singer and the obstacles of modern day romance.

•

- Grease with John Travolta and Olivia Newton John. A romantic musical about the adventures, friendships and romances of a bunch of high school kids growing up in the 50's. Here is another one you will want to see over and over. The music is fantastic and the acting is superb . It will make you wish you grew up in the 50's, poodle skirt and all. You can keep your greasy hair .

•

- **American Graffiti with Harrison Ford, Richard Dreyfess, Ron Howard and a plethora of other stars. High School grads riding the strip for one final night before adult life begins.**

-

- **The Electric Horseman with Robert Redford and Jane Fonda. A former rodeo star is reduced to doing cereal commercials atop a million dollar horse , when he finds out the horse is being drugged. He steals the horse and off he rides with a sexy reporter chasing after him and the story. Again we have Redford looking mighty fine.**

-

- **The Sting with Robert Redford and Paul Newman. Wow, now this is a classic. A small time con artist hooks up with a pro in order to seek revenge on the crime boss who murdered a friend. Together they create an elaborate scheme to make the boss pay for his deeds without him even realizing what happened.**

-

- **Butch Cassidy and The Sundance Kid with Robert Redford and Paul Newman. This is based on the true story of the Wild Bunch. A gang of bank robbers who robbed trains in the midwest for decades until they were tired of running. Along for the ride was Sundance's girlfriend. They took their wealth and moved to Argentina and brought property there. After robbing again in Argentina , they met their demise in a shootout in Bolivia. The two are buried there.**

Six

Chapter 5 : The 1980's

The 1980's

- **Top Gun with Tom Cruise, Kelly McGillis, Meg Ryan, Val Kilmer, Anthony Edwards, Tom Skerritt. A hotshot fighter pilot training at the Naval Weapons Academy manages to tick off the other students with his attitude and at the same time vies for the affection of his instructor.**

-

- Terms of Endearment with Shirley Maclaine, Jack Nicholson, Debra Winger and Jeff Daniels. A story of a bond between a mother and daughter who seem to always be at odds and the unexpected ups and downs of everyday life. Life doesn't always go as planned, but we persevere.

-

- St. Elmo's Fire with a plethora of young up and coming stars.

Seven very close friends deal with the struggles transitioning from adolescents to adults in this coming of age classic. Did you ever see a movie that just felt like you were a part of it? Well, this is that movie, I am obsessed with this one. It hit home to me in so many ways, as I graduated from college in 1985 and shared many of these experiences.

•

• An Officer and a Gentleman with Richard Gere and Debra Winger. A Naval officer who struggles with authority , learns a few tough life lessons from his instructor and his new love. He learns what things are important in life.

•

• When Harry Met Sally with Meg Ryan and Billy Crystal. Two newly college graduates argue over whether men and women can have a strictly platonic relationship, only to cross paths ten years later and put that theory to the test.

•

• Out of Africa with Meryl Streep and Robert Redford. An aristocratic plantation owner in Africa has a lengthy romance with a big game hunter. The location for this movie was gorgeous and it made you want to go there and experience the wild.

•

• The Big Chill with another plethora of stars including William Hurt, Kevin Kline, Glenn Close, Jeff Goldblum and Meg Tilley. A once very close group of friends come together to mourn the death of one of their own. Over several days they reassess their lives and disappointments and unresolved issues they had with the deceased friend. It made them realize how time gets away from us and sometimes even the people we used to cherish most.

- Steel Magnolias with Julia Roberts, Sally Field, Dolly Parton, Olympia Dukakis, Tom Sherritt, and Shirley Maclaine, among many others. A story of a group of women who are close friends and they welcome a new girl into town. Their friendship grows and perseveres through many joyous moments and many tragic ones as well.

- Moonstruck with Cher and Nicholas Cage, Olympia Dukakis and more. An Italian widow is about to marry a man that she is just friends with, until she meets his younger brother and they begin a whirlwind romance in secret. As her secret is revealed, so is another family secret. The comradery around the dinner table with this family is so hilarious and comforting at the same time. Cher is one of my favorite actresses, she has many other movies to catch also.

Chapter 6 : The 1990's

The 1990's

- **Bridges of Madison County with Clint Eastwood and Meryl Streep. This is a story about a farmer's wife who meets a photographer that comes to town to take pictures of covered bridges. A romance begins, although it is brief, they feel like they are soul mates who meet many years too late.**

-

- **Titanic with Leonardo DeCaprio and Kate Winslet. The true story of the maiden voyage of the ship the Titanic and the lives of those on that ship that hit an iceberg and sank . It focuses on the short romance of two of the passengers.**

-

- **Ghost with Patrick Swayze and Demi Moore. A lovely romance between two people who just seem perfectly matched** and the tragedy that unfolds when greed and envy interrupt their life. Whoopie Goldberg has a significant role as a medium who tries to bring communication from the dead to the living. Very sweet movie, another one to have a good cry during.

•

• **Pretty Woman with Richard Gere and Julia Roberts. A very wealthy businessman encounters a prostitute while in LA. They fall in love but have many obstacles to overcome as they each have very different pasts.**

•

• **Sleepless in Seattle with Meg Ryan and Tom Hanks. A widower's young son tries to fix up his dad with a woman by calling in to a radio show and asking for help. A woman listening gets obsessed with finding the man and eventually travels across the country to find him. With a little help from the son, a romance blooms.**

•

• **When a Man Loves a Woman with Meg Ryan and Andy Garcia. A romance between a husband and wife begins to fade as she begins to drink excessively and to the point of endangering their kids. When you love someone so much you would give your life for them, that is true love. This story is about that kind of love and how a relationship survives the struggles and hardships of the life of an addict and how love wins. It isn't easy and it isn't pretty but love wins.**

•

• **Prince of Tides with Barbra Streisand and Nick Nolte. A psychiatrist falls for a patient who has endured deep lasting scars from his childhood. Childhood sexual abuse comes to light in this romantic drama, not pleasant but a fact of life.**

Learning how to open up and discuss it goes a long way for the healing process.

-

- **The Scarlet Letter with Demi Moore and Gary Oldham. From the novel of the same title, the story of a widow becoming pregnant and not naming the father. She is labeled an adulteress by the community.**

Eight

Chapter 7 : The 2000's

The 2000's

- **The Notebook with Ryan Gosling and Rachel McAdams. Set in the 1940's, two young people are in love, she is from a wealthy family and he, just a poor mill worker. When he goes off to war she marries another, only to have that old flame rekindled when he returns from the war. Their love story survives through the decades.**

-

- **Slumdog Millionaire with Dev Patel and Freida Pinto. A young man living in Mumbai, in a last ditch effort to find the woman he loves, goes on a game show in hopes that she will be watching and try to find him. Filmed in India, it won eight Academy Awards. This one is a must see.**

-

- The Curious Case of Benjamin Button with Brad Pitt and Cate Blanchett. This story begins with a baby being born with an aging disease, who is taken in by a nurse who cares for the elderly. The movie follows his life throughout his disease as he gets younger through the years. He encounters one woman that he falls in love with and hopes that one day they will meet again when they are the same age. What an awesome story!

-

- P.S. I Love you with Hiliary Swank and Gerard Butler. A young woman who just lost her husband due to an illness, starts receiving letters after he is gone. These letters are from him , which he wrote before his passing, and have them delivered to her in the months that follow. It is his way of trying to soothe her pain and help her move on with her life. Bring out the tissues for this one.

-

- What Women Want with Mel Gibson and Helen Hunt. I love my Mel Gibson and he shines in this little romance. He is a male chauvinist who can hear what women are thinking. Naturally he uses this new skill to his advantage by trying to use it against his new female boss. After his scheme to get her fired begins to progress, he finds himself falling in love with her.

-

- The Proposal with Sandra Bullock and Ryan Reynolds. A female boss is about to lose her work visa and may face deportation back to Canada, when she comes up with a plan to marry her male assistant in order to stay. It is a cute, funny, romantic flick.

-

- A Walk to Remember with Mandy Moore and Shane West.

Another one to bring out the tissues on, when two young teens meet by chance doing community service together. She, a minister's daughter , and he, the cocky wealthy snob from school, who has made fun of her in the past. They fall in love under family protests , but eventually win them over, only to have a tragic ending to their short love affair.

•

• Revolutionary Road with Leonardo DiCaprio and Kate Winslet. This story is about the ups and downs of marriage , working through the difficulties of balancing jobs, parenting, being a spouse and finding yourself. How as the years pass, dreams and wishes seem to become impossible to achieve.

•

• Eternal Sunshine of the Spotless Mind with Jim Carrey and Kate Winslet. The story of a couple who have been together for sometime but just can't seem to make it work. So Clementine sees a psychiatrist and has a procedure done to erase her memory of Joel. When he finds this out he reacts and does the same thing, but once it begins to work and he starts to forget he suddenly realizes he does not want to lose those memories.

•

• Love Actually with an all star cast follows the lives of eight couples during the month before the Christmas holidays in London. Their lives in one way or another are intertwined with the one common element, love, and how that love reaches our friends, families, and acquaintances and creates our connection with each other.

•

•

• Conclusion : Now you have seen my favorites of all time, so get out there and start watching.

•

Nine

Conclusion

One more movie that fell into the 1930's is Gone With the Wind. Clark Gable and Vivien Leigh head up an all star cast during this Civil War picture. Mainly focusing on the southern belle who lives on a plantation and lives quite the blessed life. The movie follows her through her struggles during the Civil War and her love triangle with two men. It won eight academy awards.

This list of course is just some of my favorites and ones I have watched over and over again. I hope you can relate to many of these movies and enjoy them as much as I have. I'm sure as you can tell, I am a huge Robert Redford, Paul Newman, Meryl Streep, Meg Ryan, and Tom Hanks fan.

Movies have a way of warming our hearts and giving us hope. Some are true to life and others are what we want to be true to life.

We can learn from all of them. So, let's get to it, start that bucket list of your own. I'm going to head to the 1940's list myself and get started, I'm sure these classics will not disappoint me.

There are many ways you can view these movies; apps to download, old school VHS and DVD's, antenna TV, video libraries, or borrow from friends. Do some research and you can probably find most of these readily available. Most of them won awards and have sustained their popularity for many years. And if you are like me , you may even purchase your favorites to always have them handy on a rainy day when you need a good cry.

Maybe my next list will be Drama/Thrillers. More to come..

Afterword

Resources

Janes, D. (n.d.). *The Most Romantic Movies of All Time*. Harper's BAZAAR. Retrieved October 7, 2021,

Film, R. (2022, June 22). *The Best Romance Movies of the '50s*. Ranker. Retrieved October 7, 2022, from https://www.ranker.com/list/best-50s-romance-movies/ranker-film

I.M.B. (1996, May 30). *The Scarlet Letter (1995)*. IMDb. Retrieved July 10, 2022, from https://www.imdb.com/title/tt0114345/

https://www.imdb.com/title/tt0338013/plotsummary

Film, R. (2022b, June 22). *The Best Romance Movies of the 1960s*. Ranker. Retrieved July 10, 2022, from *https://www.ranker.com/list/best-60s-romance-movies/ranker-film*

I.M.B. (1996, May 30). *The Scarlet Letter (1995)*. IMDb. Retrieved July 10, 2022, from https://www.imdb.com/title/tt0114345/

Wiki Targeted (Entertainment). (n.d.). Oscars Wiki. Retrieved July 10, 2022, from https://oscars.fandom.com/wiki/Gone_with_the_Wind

Flickchart. (n.d.). *The Best Romance Movies of the 1970s*. Retrieved July 10, 2022, from https://www.flickchart.com/charts.aspx?genre=romance&decade=1970&perpage=50&page=2

Sampson, M. (2021, February 12). *Top 10 '70s Romance Movies*.

Ultimate Classic Rock. Retrieved July 10, 2022, from https://ulti mateclassicrock.com/70s-romance-movies/

White Christmas (1954). (1954, December 24). IMDb. Retrieved July 10, 2022, from https://www.imdb.com/title/tt0047673/?ref_ =ttls_li_tt

https://www.supersummary.com/the-notebook

https://en.wikipedia.org/wiki/

https://www.imdb.com/title/tt0421715/plotsummary#synopsi s

https://www.supersummary.com/ps-i-love-you/summary/

What Women Want - Wikipedia

http://en.wikipedia.org › wiki › What_Women_Want

Plot Summary (3) - The Proposal (2009) - IMDb

https://www.imdb.com› title › plot summary

https://www.imdb.com/title/tt0281358/plotsummary

https://en.wikipedia.org/wiki/Revolutionary_Road_(film)

Plot Synopsis - Love Actually (2003) - IMDb

https://www.imdb.com › title › synopsis>Love Actually